W9-BFR-733

For my wife and children, who are more patient than I am. And of course my parents— who are still trying to figure out what it is I do for a living.

— R. B.

An *ipicturebook* is a book you can read anywhere. Delve into the pages of the book or download it to your portable, desktop, or handheld PC by following the directions at "Free ebooks" at www.ipicturebooks.com. Please have the ISBN number of this book ready to get your free ebook of *Hide, Clyde!* The ISBN is located above the bar code on the back cover of this book.

Hide, Clyde!
ipicturebooks.com
24 W. 25th St.
New York, NY 10010
Visit us at www.ipicturebooks.com

Copyright © 2002 by Russell Benfanti

All rights reserved. No part of this book may be reproduced or transmitted in any form or by any means, electronic or mechanical, including photocopying, recording, or by any information storage and retrieval system, without permission in writing from the publisher.

ISBN 1-59019-047-5
LCCN 2001093883

10 9 8 7 6 5 4 3 2 1

TWP
Printed in Singapore

# Hide, Clyde!

## by Russell Benfanti

## ipicturebooks

New York
www.ipicturebooks.com
Distributed by Little, Brown and Company

Deep in the jungle, dangerous and wide,

Clyde and his brothers were taught how to hide.

Many creatures like chameleons to munch,

And if they see them—*ahhh! That's lunch!*

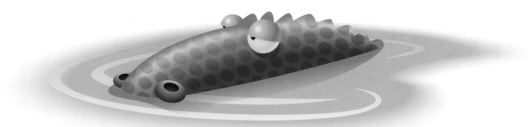

Did he hide under a rock? Up in a tree?

Chameleons change their colors.

Watch and you'll see.

His mother taught colors all night and all day,

But Clyde couldn't seem to learn the right way.

On leaves of green where he tried to hide,

Clyde changed to bright red on the outside.

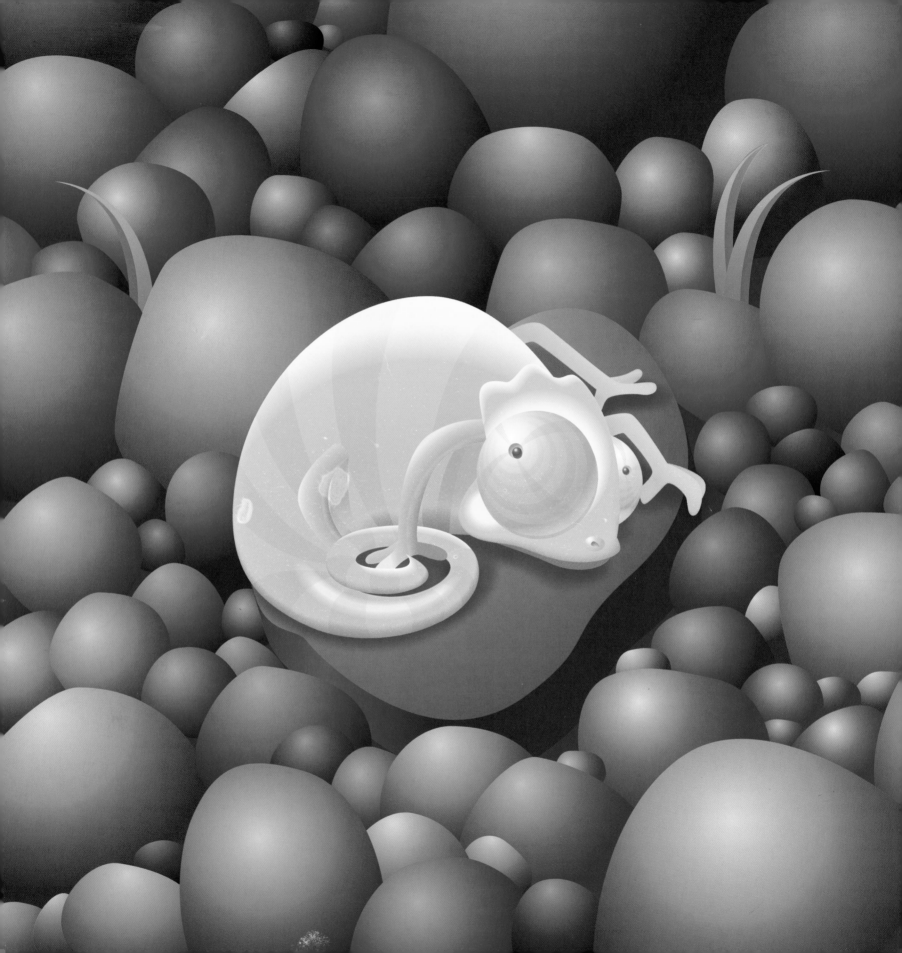

When he sat on stones shiny and blue,

He made his skin yellow. It's sad but it's true!

Orange flowers put his head in a spin.

That's when he chose purple for the color of his skin.

Now Clyde wasn't slow, or even dumb,

But when he tried to match colors,

He stood out like a sore thumb.

There was one cool thing that Clyde could do,

And that was catch bugs on his tongue,

'Cause it was covered with goo!

When he wanted a bug for a juicy snack,

He shot out his tongue and—*whack!*

Clyde could catch any bug,

Fat or thin, big or small.

This he could do. He could catch them all.

One day while Clyde was showing off his gift,

He tried to zap a bee, and it gave him a lift!

Clyde pulled back but couldn't do a thing,

And soon Clyde and the bee had taken wing.

Up the bee flew, high and away,

They traveled a long time, for almost a day.

Then over a place that Clyde did not know,

His tongue decided to simply let go.

He tumbled down into a house on the ground,

Without even a chance to look around.

Stuck in a strange room, trapped inside,

All Clyde had to do was hide!

Clyde heard something coming into the room.

Where could he hide to avoid his doom?

When he looked around for a leaf or a rock,

All he could find was a pink polka-dot sock.

Clyde was scared.

This was what his mother taught.

If he didn't change now,

He'd certainly be caught.


Clyde tried and tried with all of his might,

And then all of a sudden . . . he was out of sight.

He did it! He did it! Clyde could finally hide.

But he still had to find his way outside.

Clyde could blend with any color, pattern, or trim—

This was lots of fun, 'cause no one could see him.

He hid in some buttons and then on a shoe,

It was amazing, the matching that Clyde could now do!

He could look like a sign or blend with a label.

Clyde had no fear—now that he was able.

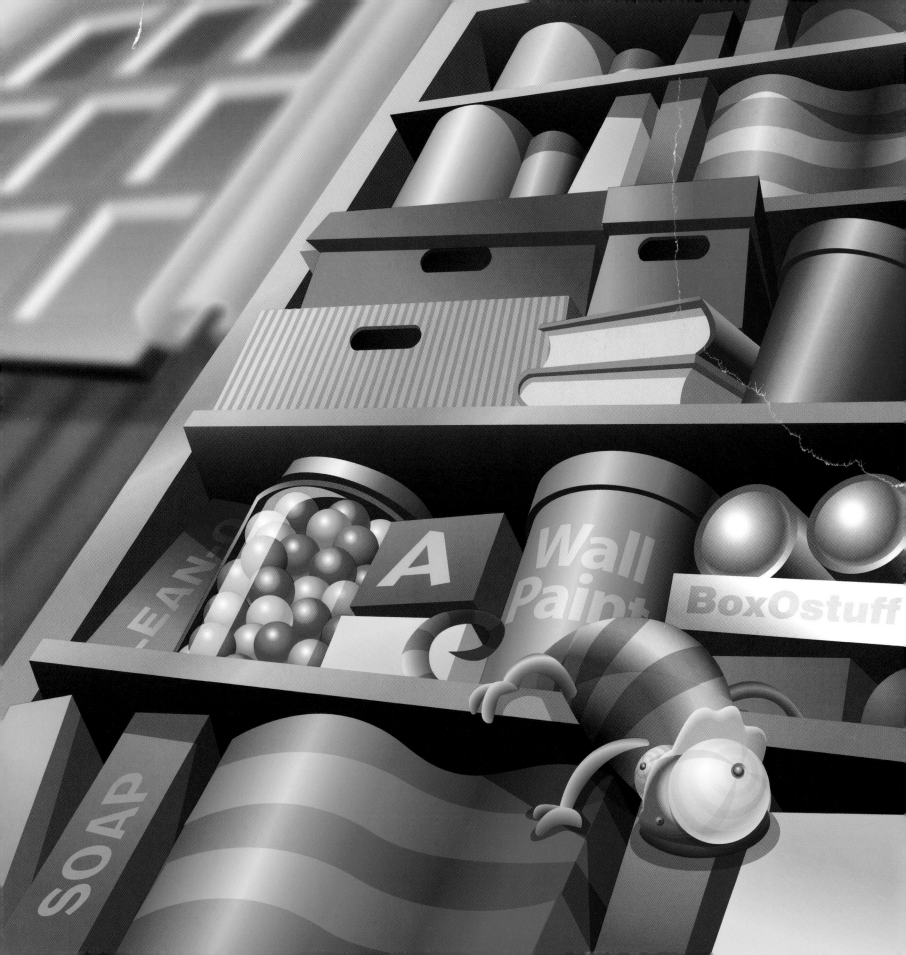

He scampered toward the window, then ran some more,

Suddenly he found what he was looking for.

He liked that room. It helped him to hide.

But beyond the window was the outside!

He climbed to the window and what did he see?

That same yellow bumble sitting in a tree.

The bee told Clyde she was heading for home.

Did he want a lift or to stay there alone?

It took no time at all for Clyde to decide,
And he climbed up for the long, long ride.